MOG TIME
Six stories about Mog

written and illustrated by
Judith Kerr

TED SMART

For Ian Craig
the best art editor in the business
with love and thanks

This edition produced for The Book People Ltd,
Hall Wood Avenue, Haydock, St Helens WA11 9UL
First published in hardback in Great Britain
by HarperCollins Children's Books in 2004
10 9 8 7 6 5 4 3 2 1
ISBN: 0-00-772596-5

Contents

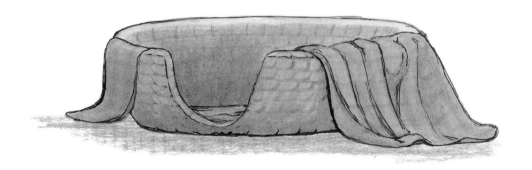

MOG
the Forgetful Cat

For our own Mog

Mr Thomas

Mrs Thomas

Nicky

Debbie

Once there was a cat called Mog.
She lived with a family called Thomas.
Mog was nice but not very clever.
She didn't understand a lot of things.
A lot of other things she forgot.
She was a very forgetful cat.

Sometimes she ate her supper.
Then she forgot that she had
eaten it.

Sometimes she thought of something
in the middle of washing her leg.
Then she forgot to wash the rest of it.

Once she forgot
that cats can't fly.

But most of all she forgot her cat flap.
The cat flap led from the kitchen
into the garden.
Mog could go out…

…and in
again.
It was
her
own
little
door.

The garden always made Mog very excited.
She smelled all the smells.
She chased the birds.
She climbed the trees.
She ran round and round
with a big fluffed-up tail.
And then she forgot the cat flap.
She forgot that she had a cat flap.
She wanted to go back into the house,
but she couldn't remember how.

In the end she sat outside the kitchen window
and meowed until someone let her in.

Afterwards you could always tell
where she had sat.
This made Mr Thomas very sad.
He said, "Bother that cat!"
But Debbie said, "She's nice!"

Once Mog had a very bad day.
Even the start of the day was bad.
Mog was still asleep.
Then Nicky picked her up.
He hugged her
and said, "Nice kitty!"
Mog said nothing.
But she was not happy.

Then it was breakfast time.
Mog forgot that cats have milk for breakfast.
She forgot that cats only have eggs as a treat.

She ate an egg for her breakfast.
Mrs Thomas said, "Bother that cat!"
Debbie said, "Nicky doesn't like eggs anyway."

Mog looked through her cat flap.
It was raining in the garden.
Mog thought, "Perhaps the sun is shining in the street."
When the milkman came she ran out.
The milkman shut the door.

The sun was not shining in the street after all.

It was raining.

A big dog came down the street.

Mog ran.

The dog ran too.

Mog ran right round the house.
And the dog ran after her.
She climbed over the fence.
She ran through the garden
and jumped up outside the kitchen window.
She meowed a big meow,
very sudden and very loud.

Mrs Thomas said, "Bother that cat!"
Debbie said, "It wasn't her fault."

Mog was very sleepy.
She found a nice warm, soft place
and went to sleep.
She had a lovely dream.
Mog dreamed that she had wings.

She could fly everywhere.
She could fly faster than the birds,
even quite big birds…
Suddenly she woke up.

Mrs Thomas said, "Bother that cat!"
Debbie said, "I think you look nicer without a hat."

Debbie gave Mog her supper
and Mog ate it all up.
Then Debbie and Nicky went to bed.

Mog had a rest too,
but Mr Thomas wanted to see the fight.
Mr Thomas said, "Bother that cat!"

Mog thought, "Nobody likes me."
Then she thought, "Debbie likes me."
Debbie's door was open.

Debbie's bed was warm.
Debbie's hair was soft, like kitten fur.
Mog forgot that Debbie was not a kitten.

Debbie had a dream.
It was a bad dream.
It was a dream about a tiger.

The tiger wanted
to eat Debbie.
It was licking her hair.

Debbie shouted.
Mog jumped.
Mr and Mrs Thomas said,
"Bother, bother,
BOTHER that cat!"
Debbie said nothing.
She was still crying
because of the bad dream.

Mog ran out of the room
and right through the house
and out of her cat flap.
She was very sad.
The garden was dark.
The house was dark too.
Mog sat in the dark
and thought dark thoughts.
She thought, "Nobody likes me.
They've all gone to bed.
There's no one to let me in.
And they haven't even given me my supper."

Then she noticed something.
The house was not quite dark.
There was a little light moving about.
She looked through the window
and saw a man in the kitchen.
Mog thought, "Perhaps that man will let me in.
Perhaps he will give me my supper."

She meowed her biggest meow,
very sudden and very, very loud.
The man was surprised.
He dropped his bag.
It made a big noise
and everyone in the house woke up.

Mr Thomas ran down to the kitchen
and shouted, "A burglar!"
The burglar said, "Bother that cat!"
Mrs Thomas telephoned the police.
Debbie let Mog in
and Nicky hugged her.

A policeman came and they told him what had happened.
The policeman looked at Mog.
He said, "What a remarkable cat.

I've seen watch-dogs, but never a watch-cat.
She will get a medal."
Debbie said, "I think she'd rather have an egg."

Mog had a medal.

She also had an egg every day for breakfast.

Mr and Mrs Thomas told all their friends about her.

They said, "Mog is really remarkable."

And they never – (or almost never) – said, "Bother that cat!"

MOG
and Bunny

For Lucy and Alexander

One day Mog got a present.
"Here you are, Mog," said Nicky.
"This is for you. It's called Bunny."

Mog liked Bunny.

She carried him about.

She played with him…

and played with him…

and played…

and played…

and played with him.

He was her best thing.

When Mog came to have her supper,
Bunny came too.

Sometimes Mog thought
Bunny would like a drink.

But Bunny wasn't very good at drinking.
"Oh dear," said Debbie. "Look where
Bunny's got to."

And she put him on the radiator to dry.

At night Bunny slept with Mog in her basket.

During the day, when Mog was busy,
she always put Bunny somewhere nice.
You never knew where Bunny would get to.

Sometimes Bunny liked to be quiet and cosy,

and sometimes he liked to be where there was a lot going on.

Mr and Mrs Thomas didn't understand this.
They didn't say, "Look where Bunny's got to."
They shouted, "Yukk!"

They yelled, "Arrgh! What a horrible, dirty thing!"

And they threatened
to throw Bunny away
in the dustbin.

One day Mr Thomas said,
"Let's have supper in the garden."

Everyone helped to carry things out of the house.

It was a lovely supper.

But suddenly…

...there was a crash of thunder and it poured with rain.

"Quick! Inside!" shouted Mrs Thomas. "It's bedtime anyway."

"Where's Mog?"
said Debbie.
"I expect she's keeping
dry under a bush,"
said Mrs Thomas.
"She'll come in later."

In the middle of the night,
Debbie and Nicky
woke up. Mog
hadn't come
in and it was
still pouring
with rain.

"Let's go and find her," said Debbie.

It was very dark in the garden.
They shouted, "Mog! Where are you, Mog?"
But nothing happened.

Then they heard a meow.
"There she is!" shouted
Nicky. "Come on, Mog!
Come inside!"
But Mog just went
on sitting in
the rain.

It was…

dripping…

off her nose.

"What's the matter, Mog?" said Debbie.
Then she said, "Oh dear! Look where Bunny's got to."

Nicky picked Bunny up
and showed him to Mog.
"It's all right, Mog," he said.
"We've set Bunny free.
You can come inside now."

Then they carried Bunny through the dark garden…

and through the house…

and they put him on the radiator to dry.

Then they all had a big sleep.

In the morning they told Mrs Thomas
what had happened, and how Mog had
stayed with Bunny in the dark and the rain.

Debbie said, "You won't really throw
Bunny away in the dustbin, will you?"
Mrs Thomas said, "No, never. It would
make Mog too sad."

Then she sighed and said, "Perhaps Bunny is not
quite so horrible, now he's been washed by the rain."
They all looked on the radiator.

But this is where Bunny had got to.

MOG'S
Bad Thing

For Tom
with all my love

One day Mog was coming home to her garden.
She had been on a mouse hunt all night
and she was very tired.
Mog thought, "I need a big sleep."

But first she went round her garden
to see if it was just as she'd left it.
The grass was still there.

The flowers were still there.

The tree was still there, and so
was her lavatory behind the tree.
Mog thought, "That's all right then."

It was starting to rain, so she went
into the house.

Mr Bunce from the pet shop was there with Mr Thomas.
He said, "Hullo Mog. All ready for the cat show tomorrow?"
Debbie said, "There's going to be a cat show in our garden,
Mog, and you can be in it."
"What if it rains?" said Nicky. "All the cats will get wet."
"No," said Mr Bunce, "because I'm going to put up a big tent
and the cat show will be inside it."

Debbie said, "Perhaps Mog will win a prize."
Mr Thomas looked at Mog and Mog looked back at him.
He said, "Well... well, you never know."

Mog had her breakfast and went to have her big sleep.
It was a very big sleep. It was so big that she only
woke up after everyone else had gone to bed.
Mog thought, "Now for another mouse hunt."

But when she looked out she had a terrible shock.
Her garden had disappeared. The grass had disappeared.
The flowers had disappeared. The tree had disappeared
and, worst of all, so had her lavatory behind the tree.

Instead, there in the dark was a big white flappy-floppy thing.
The flappy-floppy thing moved in the wind. It went
flap! flap! flap! It went flap! flap! flap! with a loud
flappy noise. Mog thought, "I'd better run."
Then she thought, "But I want my lavatory."
Suddenly the flappy-floppy thing flapped right at her.
It nearly caught her nose. Mog ran.

She ran back into her house.

She ran through all the rooms in case the flappy-floppy thing was coming after her.

She thought, "What shall I do?

What shall I do?"

And then Mog did a bad thing.
She did not mean to do it, but she did it.
She did it in Mr Thomas's chair.

Then she hid under the sofa where
the flappy-floppy thing couldn't
get her. She was too upset to
think any more, so she went
back to sleep.

She woke up in the morning to a great noise.
It was a shouting noise and Mr Thomas was doing the shouting.
He shouted, "Look what that horrible cat has done in my chair!
Where is that horrible cat? Just wait till I find her!"

Mog did not want Mr Thomas to find her.
When no one was looking she ran out from under the sofa
and out of the room and to the very top of the house.

She thought, "No one will ever find me here.
I'll stay here for ever and ever and I'll never
go downstairs again." She was very sad.

But downstairs they
were all too busy
to think about Mog.
Mr Bunce had come
to get ready for
the cat show.
He fixed a hole in
the tent where rain
was coming through.

Then he put out a table for the cats to sit on

and chairs for the cats' people.

Debbie said,
"It's time Mog
got ready too.
Where is she?"

No one had seen her. They all shouted, "Mog! Where are you, Mog?"

Mrs Thomas said, "Oh dear, here come
the first cats for the cat show."

But there was no Mog. Then they looked in every place they could think of. But still there was no Mog.

Debbie said, "But we can't start the cat show without Mog."
"Don't worry," said Mr Bunce. "I expect she'll suddenly appear and surprise us all."

There was no time to go on looking
for Mog because more cats were arriving.
There was the Siamese from round the corner
and Blackie from the High Street
and Ginger from the paper shop
and old Mr Ben's Tommy
and Fluffy who had
once bitten Mog's ear
and Oscar who ate three
tins of cat food every day,
and a whole lot of others.

They all went into the big tent. The cats looked at each other and the cats' people looked at each other and at each others' cats. There was a prize for the most unusual cat in the show and everyone wondered which cat would win.

A lot of people thought Fluffy was unusual.
"He's only unusual as an ear biter," said Nicky.

Mr Bunce went round making notes. He could not make notes about Mog because she was not there. "Wherever can she be?" said Debbie.

Mog was getting bored with her hiding place.
She thought she'd look out of the window.
The flappy-floppy thing had stopped flapping.
It did not look so bad in daylight.

And there was her tree! It was there! It was still there! Mog thought,
"I could jump down on the flappy-floppy thing and into my garden."
Then she thought, "But it might flap at me." Then she thought, "Shall I?"

Inside the tent, Mr Bunce had finished making notes.
He said, "It's time to choose the winner of the show.
We can choose Bertie who has unusual eyes, or Oscar
who is unusually big, or Fluffy who is unusually furry,
or Min who is unusually... well, unfurry, or Mrs Pussy

who has had a very unusual number of kittens..."
But something was wrong. Fluffy was getting wet.
It was raining on Fluffy. It was raining inside the tent.
"Oh dear," said Mr Bunce. "It's another hole in the roof.
The rain *will* come through."

But then something more
than rain came through.

It was something furry.
It was something stripy.
Nicky shouted, "It's Mog!"

"Well I never," said Mr Bunce. "And in a little dress!
I thought Mog might surprise us but this beats everything."
Mog tried to say something but only a very small noise
came out. Meow! Then Mr Bunce said, "In this show we
have seen some unusual cats, but none as unusual as Mog.
She has flown through the air like a circus cat. She is an
abro-cat... I mean acrobat. She has amazed us all and
I think the prize for the most unusual cat should go to Mog."

Everyone clapped and cheered.

Well, almost everyone.

Mog got a very special prize and
Mr and Mrs Thomas got a certificate.

They were very proud. Mr Thomas was so proud that he was no longer cross about his chair. And when everyone had gone home Mr Bunce took his tent away again and Mog's garden reappeared.

It was all there just as before. The grass was there.
The flowers were there. The tree was there, and so was
her lavatory behind the tree. She was very happy.

MOG
and the Baby

For Ben Davis
who is very fond of cats

One day Mog was playing with Nicky.

Debbie was going to school.
Mr Thomas was going to work,
but Nicky had a cold.

Mog and Nicky played
Catch the String.

Then they played Bad Dogs.

Then they played Tickle Mog's Tummy,

and then they played ball.

Suddenly they heard a noise.
It was a crying noise.
It was a very loud crying noise.

Mrs Thomas said, "Look who's here.
Mrs Clutterbuck has brought us her baby.
We're going to look after it while she goes shopping."

The baby looked at Mog
and stopped crying.
It said Psss instead.

"It's trying to say puss,"
said Mrs Thomas.

"Will my baby be all right with your cat?" said Mrs Clutterbuck.

"Oh yes," said Mrs Thomas. "Mog loves babies."

But Mog and Nicky had to stop playing ball because the baby did not know how to play.

"I've got a very good idea,"
said Mrs Thomas. "Let's take
the baby for a ride in the pram."

The baby liked riding in the pram.
It said Psss.
"I've got a baby in a pram too," said Nicky.
Mog said nothing, but she was not happy.

When they came back it was lunch time.
But the baby did not want to eat its lunch.
It said Psss instead.

It said Psss and cried.
It cried so much that Mog did not
want to eat her lunch either.

She went away
and sat in her basket.

She sat in her basket
and tried to think of
other things, while
Mrs Thomas and Nicky
cleared the dishes.

The baby found a dish
to clear, too.

"Look what it's done," said Nicky.

"Oh dear,"
said Mrs Thomas.
"Perhaps the baby
would like a rest."

But the baby did
not want a rest.
It said Psss Psss Psss.
It said Psss and cried.

"It wants Mog,"
said Mrs Thomas.

"Will Mog be all right
with the baby?" said Nicky.

"Oh yes," said Mrs Thomas, "Mog loves babies."

Mog sat in her basket, and the baby stopped crying.
It was nice and quiet when the baby stopped crying.
It was so quiet that Mog fell asleep.

She had a dream.
It was a lovely dream.
It was a dream about babies.

SUDDENLY... she woke up.

Mog thought,
this baby is everywhere.

She thought,
I'm getting out.

Mog ran across the road,

but the baby was coming after her,

and a bad dog was waiting
on the other side,

and there was a car coming.

"There's my baby!" shouted Mrs Clutterbuck.
"There's Mog!" shouted Debbie.
There's only one way to go,
thought Mog, and she jumped.
She jumped away from the dog.
She jumped away from the car.
She bumped into the baby.
The baby flew through the air
and came down on the pavement.
It said Psss.
Mr Thomas stopped the car just in time.

"My baby! Oh, my baby!" said Mrs Clutterbuck.

"It's a silly baby," said Nicky.

"It shouldn't have run into the road."

"Mog saved it," said Debbie.

"She is a very brave cat," said Nicky.

"She is the bravest cat in the world. She is a baby-saving cat, and she should have a reward."

They all went to get Mog a reward.
It was a very big reward.
It was a reward from Mrs Clutterbuck.

"Mog saved my baby from being run over,"
said Mrs Clutterbuck.
"I told you," said Mrs Thomas, "Mog loves babies."

MOG
on Fox Night

For Daniel, Rebecca
Katie and Rachelle

One day Mog did not want to eat her supper.
It was fish. But Mog always had an egg for breakfast.
She thought, "Why shouldn't I have an egg for supper as well?"
She looked at the fish. Then she looked at Mrs Thomas.
She made a sad face. "Oh dear," said Mrs Thomas.
"Perhaps that fish isn't very nice."

"I'll give her some kitty food," said Nicky.
Mog looked at the kitty food. Then she looked at Nicky.
She made an even sadder face.

"I know," said Debbie. "She wants an egg."
Just then Mr Thomas came in from the garden.

Mr Thomas had been putting the binbags out
for the binmen to take away in the morning.
Mr Thomas did not like doing the binbags.
He liked it even less when it was snowing,
and he was cross.

He said, "You spoil that cat. That cat has
been given two suppers and has left them both.
She is not to be given an egg as well.
In fact, if that cat does not eat every bit
of those two suppers, she will not get
an egg for her breakfast either."
And he put the egg back in the fridge.

Mog was very sad when the egg went back in the fridge.
She was also very cross. She hissed at Mr Thomas.
Then she hissed at the fridge.

And then
she ran
through her
cat flap
and out into
the garden.

The garden was very cold.
There was snow everywhere.

But there was no snow under the binbags.
Mog crept under a binbag and went to sleep.

Debbie and Nicky were sad too when they went to bed.
"Mog never eats anything she doesn't like," said Debbie.
"She'll never eat that fish and the kitty food."
"And then she won't get an egg for her breakfast,"
said Nicky. "She'll be so cross."

Mog was cross even in her sleep.

She had a cross dream.
It was a dream about Mr Thomas.
Mr Thomas had put all the eggs
in the world into a binbag.
He wanted to take the binbag away.
Mog tried to stop him…

Suddenly she woke up.
There was snow all over her.
The binbag had gone.
Had Mr Thomas taken it away?

She looked.
Then she thought, "This is too much.
First they give me a horrible supper,
and now there's a fox in my garden."
The fox had made a hole in the binbag
and was pulling things out of it.
"What is he doing?" thought Mog.

The fox ate one of the things
he had pulled out of the binbag.
It was a chicken bone.

Then he ate something else.
It was a piece of fish.
Mog knew that piece of fish.
She had left it in her dish the day before.
It had not been nice then.
She thought, "That fox is mad."

Then she saw something else.
The fox had a little fox.
No, he had two little foxes.
He was giving them bits to eat
out of the binbag.

But one of the little foxes
only wanted to play.

It played with the snow.

It played with a twig.

It played with an old tin.

And then it wanted to play with Mog.

Mog thought, "I don't want to play with that little fox," and she ran through her cat flap and back into the house.

But the little fox ran after her.

And the other little fox ran after the first little fox.

And the big fox ran after them both.

Mog thought, "This is really too much.
First they give me a horrible supper.
Then there's a fox in my garden,
and now there are three foxes in my kitchen."

The foxes liked Mog's kitchen.
They liked the sink.

They liked the pots and pans.

They
liked
the
kitchen
cupboard,

and the breakfast table and Mog's basket.
Mog thought, "There are too many foxes here.
I'm going!"

She found a much nicer
place and went to sleep.

Very early in the morning she woke up.
Debbie woke up too.

Debbie said, "Look who's in my bed.
Why aren't you in your basket, Mog?"
Nicky said, "I wonder if she's eaten her supper."

They went down to the kitchen to see.
Mog's two dishes were empty.
"She's eaten it!" said Nicky.

Then they saw something else.
"I don't think it was Mog who ate it," said Debbie.

The foxes thought it was time to go home.
They ran out through the cat flap.

Then they ran off through the garden.
It had stopped snowing and it was a lovely day.

Debbie and Nicky
tidied the kitchen.

They tidied up every bit.

"Now you can go back in
your basket, Mog," said Nicky.
Just then Mr and Mrs Thomas came in.
Mr Thomas looked at the empty dishes.
"There," he said. "What a good cat.
I knew Mog would eat her supper in the end."

Debbie and Nicky said nothing.
After all, they thought, no one really
knew *who* had eaten Mog's supper.

Mog had

a lovely egg

for her breakfast.

She was very pleased.

And the foxes were pleased too.

MOG'S
Christmas

For my friend Mrs Cleghorn

One day Mog woke up
and nothing was right in her house.

Everybody was busy.
Debbie was busy.

Nicky was busy.

Mr and Mrs Thomas
were busy.

And there were too many
people in the house.

There was a jolly uncle

...and two aunts
on tippy-toe.

Mog thought, "I don't like it here."
She went and sat outside on the window-sill.
There was nothing to do and no one to play
with, so after a while she went back to sleep.

Suddenly she woke up.
She saw something.
It was a tree.
It was a tree walking.

Mog thought, "Trees don't walk.
Trees should stay in one place.
Once trees start walking about
anything might happen."
She ran up the side of the
house in case the tree should
come and get her.
"Come down," shouted the tree.
"Come down, Mog!"
"First it walks," thought Mog,
"and now it's shouting at me.
I do not like that tree at all."
And she ran right up to the roof.

The tree went on shouting for a while.
Then it went into the house.
Mog stayed on the roof.
Some white things fell out of the sky.
Some fell on the roof and some fell
on Mog.
They were very cold.

At supper time
Mog was still on the roof.
"She must have her supper,"
said Debbie. "Mog always
has her supper."
Mrs Thomas gave Mog her supper.
But still Mog did not come down.

In the morning Mog did not come down either.
She had found a nice tall place, and she
was asleep.
She was having a lovely dream.

Mog dreamed that she was sitting on a cloud.
Some white things were falling out of the sky.
Mog tried to catch them. She was very happy.
But suddenly the cloud began to melt...

Inside the house everyone was sad
because Mog would not come down.
They were too sad to eat their breakfast.

Even the jolly uncle was sad,
and one of the aunts cried.

Suddenly there was a noise.
It was a noise in the chimney.
And then something came down it.
It came right down the chimney and
fell into the fireplace with a thump.

"It's Father Christmas!"
cried one of the aunts.
"No, dear," said the other aunt,
"Father Christmas does not
have a tail."

Debbie cried, "It's Mog!"

Mog had to have a bath.
But then...

Then everything was lovely.
The whole house was lovely.
The tree had stopped walking
about and had made itself
all pretty.

And Mog had three boiled eggs and
some turkey and a present to unwrap.

"Happy Christmas, Mog," said Debbie.